Monsters, Myths & Mysteries

A TANGLED TOUR MAZE BOOK

Paul M. Woodruff

Sterling Publishing Co., Inc.
New York

For Dennis, Dan, and Scott, the living legends.
And for Craig, a member of the Bigfoot Rumor Busters.

10 9 8 7 6 5 4 3 2 1

Published by Sterling Publishing Co., Inc.
387 Park Avenue South, New York, NY 10016
© 2007 by Paul M. Woodruff
Distributed in Canada by Sterling Publishing
c/o Canadian Manda Group, 165 Dufferin Street
Toronto, Ontario, Canada M6K 3H6
Distributed in the United Kingdom by GMC Distribution Services
Castle Place, 166 High Street, Lewes, East Sussex, England BN7 1XU
Distributed in Australia by Capricorn Link (Australia) Pty. Ltd.
P.O. Box 704, Windsor, NSW 2756, Australia

Printed in China

Sterling ISBN-13: 978-1-4027-3803-6
       ISBN-10: 1-4027-3803-X

For information about custom editions, special sales, premium and
corporate purchases, please contact Sterling Special Sales
Department at 800-805-5489 or specialsales@sterlingpub.com.

Contents

Introduction

Bigfoot, the Loch Ness Monster, and other mysterious creatures that you may know of lurk within these pages. But have you heard of the Kappa, the Chupacabra, or the Lambton Worm? In the following pages, you'll discover all these and much more.

Each full-color illustration is a challenging maze. To solve each one, first find the arrow that points to the maze entrance. Then see if you can avoid the numerous dead ends and reach the exit arrow. The correct path may cross through different colored objects or creatures—just don't cross any black lines. The mazes vary in difficulty, but the answers are provided in back, just in case.

So grab a pencil, tackle the mazes, and learn about monster tales from various cultures, beasts of ancient mythology, and recent sightings of the unexplained as you take a tangled tour through the world of monsters, myths, and mysteries.

Paul M. Woodruff

Aliens

Despite countless reported sightings of both extra-terrestrials and their ships, no proof has yet been found of visitors from other planets. Still, many people believe *aliens* exist; others say that Earth is the only planet with living beings.

Atlantis

The fabled city of *Atlantis*, and the great island that it occupied, allegedly sank beneath the ocean thousands of years ago during a catastrophic day of earthquakes and tidal waves. To this day, explorers still search for clues as to whether Atlantis actually existed.

Baba Yaga

Baba Yaga is a witch from Russian folktales. Villainous in some tales, at other times she offers wise advice to those brave enough to face her. She dwells in the deep forest in a small hut that, bizarrely enough, stands on giant chicken legs.

Bigfoot

Are these creatures an unknown ape species, an ancient race of humans, or just a hoax? Many people claim *Bigfoot* roams America's Pacific Northwest forests. Eyewitnesses report similar huge hairy creatures—generally said to be eight to ten feet tall—in Asia, Australia, and other parts of the United States and Canada.

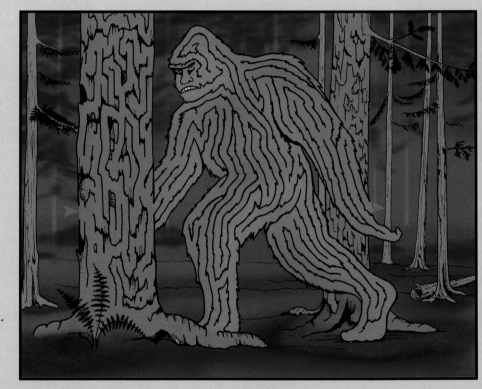

Black Dogs

Black dogs are ghostly creatures said to haunt lonely British roads and cemeteries. They have the ability to appear and vanish at will, and are sometimes described as having huge fiery red eyes.

Bunyip

The Australian *bunyip* has been said to possess tusks, wings, fur, scales, or various combinations of these traits. Aboriginal tales often describe the bunyip as a large, fearsome, water-dwelling beast.

Camelot

Camelot was the kingdom inhabited by King Arthur and his Knights of the Round Table. Although numerous legends recount their adventures, whether King Arthur or Camelot ever actually existed is still debated by many.

Centaurs

The myths and legends of ancient Greece were full of fantastic creatures. Many of them were bizarre combinations of other well-known animals. The *centaurs*—part horse, part man—were known as wise but savage warriors.

Chupacabra

Witnesses say that this chimpanzee-size creature preys on livestock at night, draining blood from its victims like a vampire. Recent sightings of the *chupacabra* have been reported in Mexico, Puerto Rico, and Chile.

Cyclopes

In Greek mythology, the *Cyclopes* were a race of one-eyed giants who farmed crops and kept flocks of immense sheep. They were a danger to any human who traveled through their homeland. The Greek hero Odysseus was famed for having outsmarted a Cyclops that had trapped his crew in its lair.

Dragons

Europeans generally depict *dragons* as huge, sinister, fire-breathing monsters, quick to devour people. In the Orient, however, dragons are often regarded as honorable creatures and signs of good fortune.

Easter Island "Moai"

Hundreds of giant stone statues known as *"moai"* stand guard around tiny Easter Island in the southern Pacific Ocean. They may have been carved as guardians or perhaps as memorials to past chieftains, but no one knows for sure.

Genies

Genies are often portrayed as magical spirits who are confined to oil lamps or other enchanted items. The traveler who stumbles upon one of these items and releases the genie may be granted wishes in return. Though this would seem to be an incredible stroke of good luck, wishes that aren't carefully worded can result in disaster.

Gnomes

Gnomes are tiny folk, common in fairy tales, which dwell in the forests and meadows. They are generally seen as kind caretakers of nature and exhibit a special friendship with the animals of the area.

Grendel

The immensely powerful *Grendel* was a marsh-dwelling monster that terrorized the Danish King Hrothgar and his subjects in the ancient poem *Beowulf*. Beowulf, the hero, travels from his home in present-day Sweden to defeat the monster, repaying a debt owed to the king. After a grueling struggle, Beowulf succeeds, only to face Grendel's even more terrifying mother soon afterward.

hippogriff

A popular monster of ancient mythology, the front of the *Hippogriff* looked like an eagle and the back looked like a horse. The Hippogriff was commonly depicted on shields and banners as a sign of bravery and dignity.

Jersey Devil

Bat wings, a horse-like head, a long neck, and a dragon's tail are some of the features attributed to the *Jersey Devil*. Inhabiting the Pine Barrens of New Jersey, its exploits have been reported by hundreds, if not thousands, of people. This monster is so popular that the New Jersey Devils hockey team is even named after it.

Kappa

Kappa are Japanese water spirits with a combination of primate and turtle features. This bizarre creature can supposedly come ashore as long as the bowl-like depression at the top of its head holds water. But if the water spills out, the kappa must retreat into its river home.

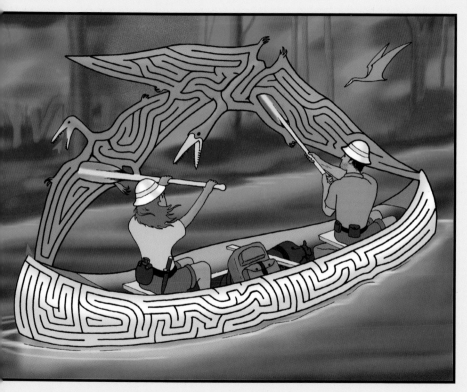

Kongamato

In the country of Zambia and surrounding nations, reports of mysterious flying creatures suggest the possibility of living pterosaurs. The *Kongamato* is described as looking like a featherless bird with a wingspread up to seven feet and a beak full of sharp teeth. It is quite a familiar sight to those that live near certain swamps and rivers which the Kongamato calls home.

Kraken

"*Kraken*" is the Scandinavian name for a huge, multi-armed sea monster that was said to be large enough to destroy ships. The tales may have been based on sightings of the giant squid or its relative, the colossal squid.

Lake Murray Beast

Lake Murray in Papua New Guinea may hold an even more imposing creature than its crocodiles. Residents have reported a large monster with legs as thick as tree trunks wading in the waters near shore. The *Lake Murray Beast* is said to resemble a prehistoric dinosaur.

Lambton Worm

Long ago, young John Lambton caught a small, eel-like creature in the river near his English home. Despite a warning not to release it, he threw it down a well. The *Lambton Worm* survived and eventually returned to the river. It grew to immense proportions and terrorized the land. Lambton returned from afar and, wearing specially-made armor, conquered the beast.

Leprechauns

Leprechauns are small, magical creatures from Irish folklore. Some stories say that a captured leprechaun will lead you to his gold. Others say that the leprechaun will grant his captor a wish or two in return for his release.

Lizard Man

In the 1970s and 1980s, the swamps of South Carolina were reputed to be the home of a ferocious *lizard man*. Red eyes, scaly skin, and clawed hands completed this creature's fearsome appearance.

Loch Ness Monster

The *Loch Ness Monster*—
Nessie—is one of the most
widely known monsters of
recent times, but it is not the
only lake monster that has been
reported. Most sightings describe
these monsters as possessing
long necks and paddle-shaped
flippers, similar to the ancient
plesiosaurs.

Loveland Frog

The *Loveland Frog* is named for a city in Ohio near where the brief sightings occurred. Reports from 1955 and 1972 describe one or more of the three-foot-tall, frog-like creatures walking upright in the roadway. Various theories include visitors from another planet or plane of existence, an unclassified animal, escaped pet monitor lizards, or simply a hoax.

Lusca

Caribbean legends tell of the *Lusca*, a huge beast with multiple arms and a bad temper that dwells in caves on the ocean floor. Could this story be based on a giant species of octopus? Octopi, generally non-aggressive by nature, tend to be bottom dwellers, so man would rarely see a giant octopus even if it did exist. That may be just fine if this particular species is as aggressive as legend states.

Manticore

From the jungles of India and Southeast Asia come tales of the vicious *manticore*. The manticore has a scorpion-like tail, the body of a lion, three rows of sharp teeth, and an almost human face.

Medusa

According to Greek mythology, *Medusa* was a creature known as a Gorgon—a being whose gaze could turn people to stone. By some accounts, she was once a beautiful woman whose hair was changed into a nest of serpents by the curse of a jealous goddess.

Mermaids

Seafarers throughout history have told tales of *mermaids* and *mermen*. In the past, songs of humpback whales and other marine creatures may have been mistaken for the music of mermaids.

Minotaur

According to Greek mythology, this huge half-man, half-bull was kept in a labyrinth by King Minos. There the *Minotaur* pursued prisoners who were forced into the maze until eventually it was killed by the hero Theseus.

Mokele-Mbembe

Could dinosaurs still roam the earth? Central Africa may hold the answers. *Mokele-mbembe*, a creature said to resemble *Apatosaurus*, is well known in the stories of the Congolese people who share its home. Creatures resembling dinosaurs have been reported from the remote parts of other continents as well.

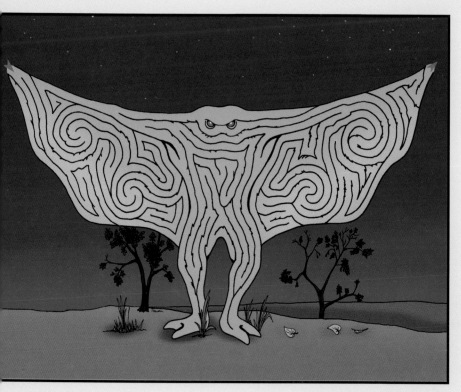

Mothman

In 1966 and 1967, sightings of a dark, mysterious creature with huge wings and glowing red eyes were reported by numerous West Virginians. The appearance of the *Mothman* was often followed by other bizarre occurrences and sightings. A similar creature known as the Owlman has also been seen in England.

Mummy's Curse

When Pharaoh Tutankhamun's tomb was discovered and opened, many believed that an ancient Egyptian curse had been awakened. This *"Mummy's Curse"* was blamed for the accidents and deaths that occurred afterwards.

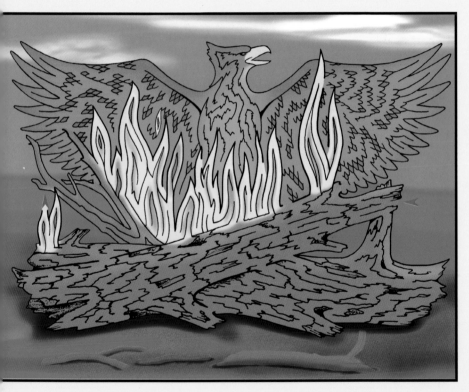

Phoenix

According to legend, the *phoenix* was a long-lived bird that was capable of being reborn. Allowing itself to be consumed by fire, the phoenix would rise again from its ashes.

Pixies

Pixies are common in folklore, especially in the British Isles. Usually depicted as miniature people with insect-like wings, they are sometimes credited with tending gardens and causing flowers to bloom.

Roc

In Arabian legends, the *roc* is an enormous bird of prey capable of carrying off elephants in its talons. Some claim that 13th century explorer Marco Polo witnessed the gigantic eggs and feathers of the roc, if not the roc itself.

Sea Serpents

Tales of monstrous *sea serpents* have existed since man first took to the open seas. The Gloucester serpent, which patrolled the waters off the Massachusetts coast in the 1800s, caused a huge splash in the newspapers of the time. Another similar creature named Caddy is said to prowl British Columbia's Cadboro Bay.

Sucuriju Gigante

In the deepest rainforests of South America, a legendary giant may lurk. Reported to reach up to 60 feet in length and to weigh several tons, the *Sucuriju Gigante* is a huge snake. It is possible that the Sucuriju is a rarely seen and even larger relative of the well-known anaconda.

Sword in Stone

According to the legend of King Arthur, the magician Merlin embedded a *sword in a stone* to find the next king of England. Only the true king would be able to pull the sword free. Arthur succeeded and inherited the crown, ruling his kingdom with the help of his Knights of the Round Table.

Thunderbirds

Could the *thunderbirds* of Native American legend be hiding in remote forests and deserts? Occasional reports of giant birds flying over Pennsylvania, Illinois, and the American West have led some believers to suggest that teratorns are responsible for thunderbird sightings. Teratorns were huge vulture-like predators that lived thousands of years ago. Others have concluded that thunderbirds may be living pterosaurs.

Trolls

Trolls and ogres are huge human-like monsters said to prey upon livestock and even humans for their meals. In Scandinavian mythology, a troll caught in direct sunlight would turn to stone.

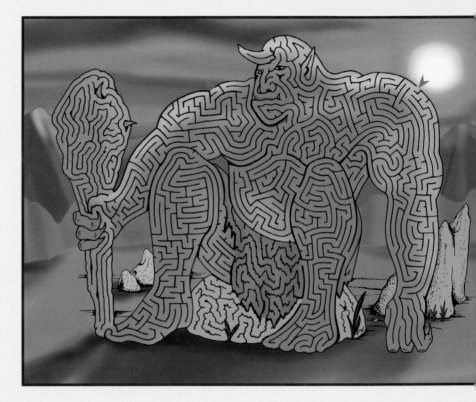

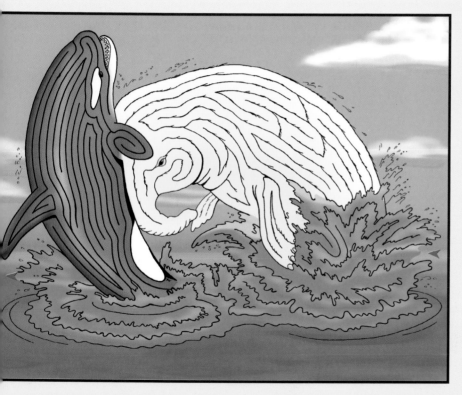

Trunko

In 1922, spectators on the South African coast claimed that a huge, unknown creature battled two whales on the surface of the Indian Ocean. The strange creature's corpse later washed up on shore and was nicknamed *Trunko*. Sporting a trunk-like snout and long, white fur, the creature was not scientifically identified before it washed out to sea again.

Unicorns

The *unicorn* is generally depicted as a white horse with a spiral horn, but it may also possess a beard, a lion's tail, or the back legs of a stag. Unicorns are often considered to have magical properties. A unicorn's horn, if dipped into a poisoned drink, is said to make the drink safe.

Vampires

Many cultures have tales of *vampires* and similar creatures, but the legends told in Eastern Europe are the basis for most Hollywood movies. These "undead" creatures prowl the night to feed on their victims. They must return to their dark resting places before sunrise as sunlight is believed to be fatal to vampires.

Werewolves

Werewolves are also known as lycanthropes. According to legend, a werewolf's bite passes the curse on. If the victim of a werewolf bite survives, he will also transform into a wolf/human hybrid at the next full moon.

Witches

In the 1600s, scores of people in the American colonies and Europe were accused of witchcraft, often on the mere suspicion of another citizen. The accused were blamed for unexplained illnesses and numerous other issues. Testimony against *witches* included such "evidence" as owning a pet cat or being seen with someone who later became ill.

Wizards

Whether known as *wizards*, sorcerers, or by some other title, most cultures have stories of those who could use potions and chants to work magic. Wizards remain a common theme in fantasy books and movies.

Wyverns

Though similar to European dragons, the two-legged *wyverns* were not usually assumed to breathe fire. In some tales, medieval Europe seems to have been plagued by numerous *wyverns* and their wingless relatives, the lindworms.

Zombies

A film industry favorite, *zombies* are based on tales from the West Indies. Although considered undead creatures like vampires, zombies have none of the ability to charm that their counterparts are sometimes credited with.

Answers

Aliens

Atlantis

Baba Yaga

Bigfoot

Black Dogs

Bunyip

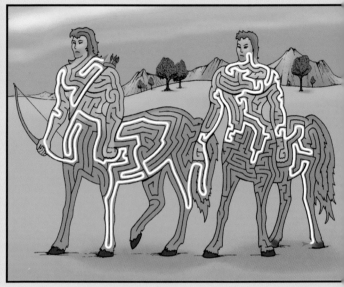

Camelot

Centaurs

Chupacabra

Cyclopes

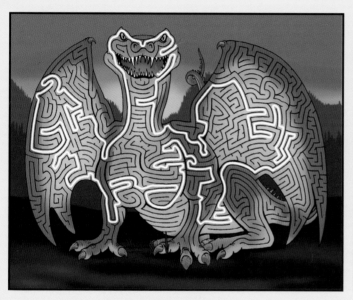

Dragons

Easter Island "Moai"

Genies

Gnomes

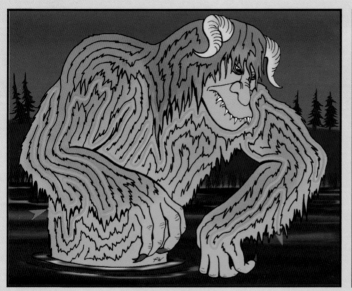

Grendel

Hippogriff

Jersey Devil

Kappa

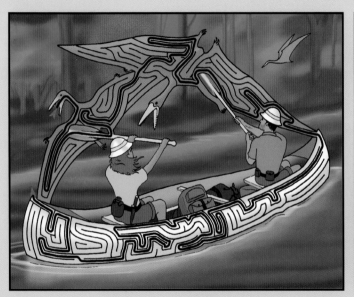

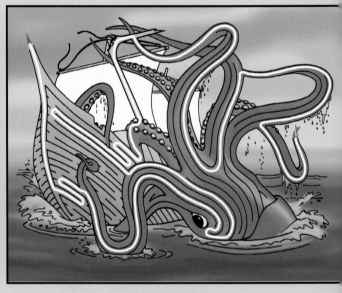

Kongamato

Kraken

Lake Murray Beast

Lambton Worm

Leprechauns

Lizard Man

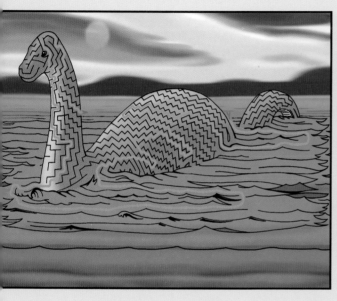

Loch Ness Monster

Loveland Frog

67

Lusca

Manticore

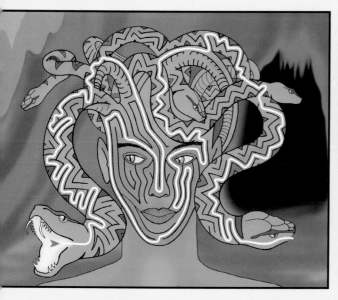

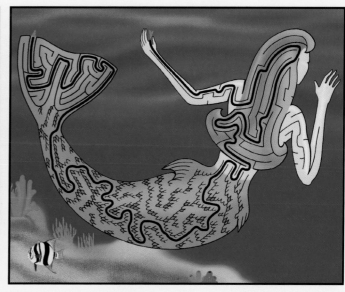

Medusa

Mermaids

Minotaur

Mokele-Mbembe

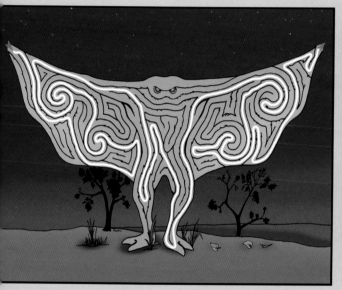

Mothman

Mummy's Curse

71

Phoenix

Pixies

Roc

Sea Serpents

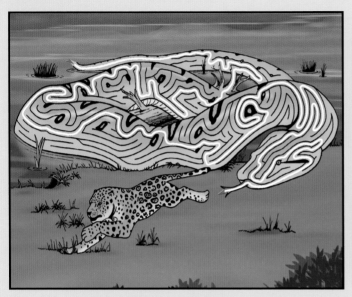

Sucuriju Gigante

Sword in Stone

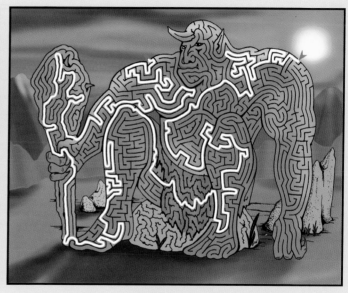

Thunderbirds

Trolls

Trunko

Unicorns

Vampires   Werewolves

Witches   Wizards

Wyverns

Zombies

Index

Pages in bold refer to answer mazes.